# THE CC
# MANIFESTO

MW01128493

# [ANNOTATED]

# by

## Karl Marx

**ISBN:** 9781981084425

Forward:

The goal of the Bonificio Masonic Library is to make the most complete and comprehensive on-line Masonic Library that produces high quality books, in an easy to read format, Masonic books both old and new, for Masons, Masonic Scholars, and just the average person with a fleeting interest in Masonry to go to fulfil their desire for Masonic Knowledge and Power.

All this of course, is a very time consuming and expensive endeavor on my part, the current library consist of over 3500 titles (and growing) that I am in the process of converting the allowable titles to Kindle format for the Modern Mason on the Go.

Any funds made from the Kindle books are directly re-invested into more books, magazines, essays and articles to provide to the community interested in Masonic Education.

The Ultimate goal of the library is to create the most complete and comprehensive virtual library on-line, where people will be able to join and go to check out the desired Masonic materials they desire, just as they can from their local libraries but without leaving the comfort of their own homes.

This however is a pipedream, which may or may never be accomplished, but a goal for the Masonic Community all the same.

My current collection consists of over 430GB of Masonic materials I have collected over the years that I would like to place into a virtual library.

Visit our website to see all available titles:
http://thegrid.ai/bonificio-masonic-library/

If you too would like to see such a dream come true, you can help to support this goal through Patreon:
https://www.patreon.com/BonificioMasonicLibrary?alert=1&ty=h

About the Bonificio Masonic Library

The Bonificio Masonic Library is an attempt to create the largest and most complete e-book library in Masonry, all funds earned from the purchase of our Kindle version books goes into the purchase, and transcription of further books so that Freemasons all over the world will have access to the necessary educational materials to develop and gain further light from Freemasonry, its symbols, history, and its meaning.

The Bonificio Masonic Library, has over 4500 books, which it is in the process of making available to every Mason, in an easy to read, and understandable format, so that you Brother, can possess all the light and knowledge available at your fingertips whenever and wherever the mood for some further light in Masonry strikes your mood.

In today's day and age, further light into the history, origins, meanings, and symbolism of our fraternity are more important than ever, and ready accessibility to the information at hand has a need for further dissemination to our Brethren where ever they may be dispersed.

So thank you for supporting us Brother's and friends of Freemasonry, and I hope you enjoy this book.

Visit our website to see all available titles:
http://thegrid.ai/bonificio-masonic-library/

Join us on Facebook:
https://www.facebook.com/groups/151584108205485
5/

The Communist Manifesto, published in 1848, is the single document most responsible for launching the often-feared political philosophy of communism. It straight up tells you to revolt against the rich, and it tells you why you should.

Here's the gist of the Manifesto, fast enough for you to read before you have to wake up and slave away at your job tomorrow: Marx describes how the bourgeoisie (the rich capitalists) rose to power over the aristocracy (kings and feudal lords), how the capitalists maintain power, and how they're now confronted by the proletariat (the working poor who are paid wages), who as communists will overthrow them. Once the proletarians take charge, they're supposed to set up a vanguard state—a temporary government to transition society from capitalism to communism. This will be a system where the most important private property—the means of production (factories, agricultural land, machinery)—will be shared in common, and no one will profit to exploit others.

Yeah, it's an incredibly controversial work. A lot of people blame the Communist Manifesto for the fact that Soviet dictator Josef Stalin put tens of millions of people into Gulags, or forced labor camps, and committed all kinds of other horrors. On the other hand, some say communism has never been implemented properly—perhaps because the continued existence of rival capitalism doesn't allow it.

Authors Karl Marx and Friedrich Engels didn't win any awards for this document, but they got a bigger prize: the manifesto, which is primarily Marx's work, is famous because it changed the world—and still does. It inspired the leaders of the Russian Revolution to overthrow the tsarist aristocracy and set up the communist Bolshevik government that led to the communist Soviet Union, one of the most powerful countries of the 20th century. China, Cuba, and other countries consider themselves communist to this day.

All that wouldn't have happened if Marx, inspired by the bad working conditions for the workforce, hadn't written this little book.

# Manifesto of the Communist Party

A spectre is haunting Europe — the spectre of communism. All the powers of old Europe have entered into a holy alliance to exorcise this spectre: Pope and Tsar, Metternich and Guizot, French Radicals and German police-spies.

Where is the party in opposition that has not been decried as communistic by its opponents in power? Where is the opposition that has not hurled back the branding reproach of communism, against the more advanced opposition parties, as well as against its reactionary adversaries?

Two things result from this fact:

I. Communism is already acknowledged by all European powers to be itself a power.

II. It is high time that Communists should openly, in the face of the whole world, publish their views, their aims, their tendencies, and meet this nursery tale of the Spectre of Communism with a manifesto of the party itself.

To this end, Communists of various nationalities have assembled in London and sketched the following manifesto, to be published in the English, French, German, Italian, Flemish and Danish languages.

## Chapter I. Bourgeois and Proletarians[1]

The history of all hitherto existing society[2] is the history of class struggles.

Freeman and slave, patrician and plebeian, lord and serf, guild-master[3] and journeyman, in a word, oppressor and oppressed, stood in constant opposition to one another, carried on an uninterrupted, now hidden, now open fight, a fight that each time ended, either in a revolutionary reconstitution of society at large, or in the common ruin of the contending classes.

---

[1] By bourgeoisie is meant the class of modern capitalists, owners of the means of social production and employers of wage labour.

By proletariat, the class of modern wage labourers who, having no means of production of their own, are reduced to selling their labour power in order to live. [Engels, 1888 English edition]

[2] That is, all written history. In 1847, the pre-history of society, the social organisation existing previous to recorded history, all but unknown. Since then, August von Haxthausen (1792-1866) discovered common ownership of land in Russia, Georg Ludwig von Maurer proved it to be the social foundation from which all Teutonic races started in history, and, by and by, village communities were found to be, or to have been, the primitive form of society everywhere from India to Ireland. The inner organisation of this primitive communistic society was laid bare, in its typical form, by Lewis Henry Morgan's (1818-1881) crowning discovery of the true nature of the gens and its relation to the tribe. With the dissolution of the primeval communities, society begins to be differentiated into separate and finally antagonistic classes. I have attempted to retrace this dissolution in The Origin of the Family, Private Property, and the State, second edition, Stuttgart, 1886. [Engels, 1888 English Edition and 1890 German Edition (with the last sentence omitted)]

[3] Guild-master, that is, a full member of a guild, a master within, not a head of a guild. [Engels, 1888 English Edition]

In the earlier epochs of history, we find almost everywhere a complicated arrangement of society into various orders, a manifold gradation of social rank. In ancient Rome we have patricians, knights, plebeians, slaves; in the Middle Ages, feudal lords, vassals, guild-masters, journeymen, apprentices, serfs; in almost all of these classes, again, subordinate gradations.

The modern bourgeois society that has sprouted from the ruins of feudal society has not done away with class antagonisms. It has but established new classes, new conditions of oppression, new forms of struggle in place of the old ones.

Our epoch, the epoch of the bourgeoisie, possesses, however, this distinct feature: it has simplified class antagonisms. Society as a whole is more and more splitting up into two great hostile camps, into two great classes directly facing each other — Bourgeoisie and Proletariat.

From the serfs of the Middle Ages sprang the chartered burghers of the earliest towns. From these burgesses the first elements of the bourgeoisie were developed.

The discovery of America, the rounding of the Cape, opened up fresh ground for the rising bourgeoisie. The East-Indian and Chinese markets, the colonisation of America, trade with the colonies, the increase in the means of exchange and in commodities generally, gave to commerce, to navigation, to industry, an impulse never before known, and thereby, to the revolutionary element in the tottering feudal society, a rapid development.

The feudal system of industry, in which industrial production was monopolised by closed guilds, now no longer sufficed for the growing wants of the new markets. The manufacturing system took its place. The guild-masters were pushed on one side by the manufacturing middle class; division of labour between the different corporate guilds vanished in the face of division of labour in each single workshop.

Meantime the markets kept ever growing, the demand ever rising. Even manufacturer no longer sufficed. Thereupon, steam and machinery revolutionised industrial production. The place of manufacture was taken by the giant, Modern Industry; the place of the industrial middle class by industrial millionaires, the leaders of the whole industrial armies, the modern bourgeois.

Modern industry has established the world market, for which the discovery of America paved the way. This market has given an immense development to commerce, to navigation, to communication by land. This development has, in its turn, reacted on the extension of industry; and in proportion as industry, commerce, navigation, railways extended, in the same proportion the bourgeoisie developed, increased its capital, and pushed into the background every class handed down from the Middle Ages.

We see, therefore, how the modern bourgeoisie is itself the product of a long course of development, of a series of revolutions in the modes of production and of exchange.

Each step in the development of the bourgeoisie was accompanied by a corresponding political advance of that class. An oppressed class under the sway of the feudal nobility, an armed and self-governing association in the medieval commune[4]: here independent urban republic (as in Italy and

---

4 This was the name given their urban communities by the townsmen of Italy and France, after they had purchased or conquered their initial rights of self-government from their feudal lords. [Engels, 1890 German edition]

"Commune" was the name taken in France by the nascent towns even before they had conquered from their feudal lords and masters local

Germany); there taxable "third estate" of the monarchy (as in France); afterwards, in the period of manufacturing proper, serving either the semi-feudal or the absolute monarchy as a counterpoise against the nobility, and, in fact, cornerstone of the great monarchies in general, the bourgeoisie has at last, since the establishment of Modern Industry and of the world market, conquered for itself, in the modern representative State, exclusive political sway. The executive of the modern state is but a committee for managing the common affairs of the whole bourgeoisie.

The bourgeoisie, historically, has played a most revolutionary part.

The bourgeoisie, wherever it has got the upper hand, has put an end to all feudal, patriarchal, idyllic relations. It has pitilessly torn asunder the motley feudal ties that bound man to his "natural superiors", and has left remaining no other nexus between man and man than naked self-interest, than callous "cash payment". It has drowned the most heavenly ecstasies of religious fervour, of chivalrous enthusiasm, of philistine sentimentalism, in the icy water of egotistical calculation. It has resolved personal worth into exchange value, and in place of the numberless indefeasible chartered freedoms, has set up that single, unconscionable freedom — Free Trade. In one word, for exploitation, veiled by religious and political illusions, it has substituted naked, shameless, direct, brutal exploitation.

The bourgeoisie has stripped of its halo every occupation hitherto honoured and looked up to with reverent awe. It has

---

self-government and political rights as the "Third Estate." Generally speaking, for the economical development of the bourgeoisie, England is here taken as the typical country, for its political development, France. [Engels, 1888 English Edition] converted the physician, the lawyer, the priest, the poet, the man of science, into its paid wage labourers.

The bourgeoisie has torn away from the family its sentimental veil, and has reduced the family relation to a mere money relation.

The bourgeoisie has disclosed how it came to pass that the brutal display of vigour in the Middle Ages, which reactionaries so much admire, found its fitting complement in the most slothful indolence. It has been the first to show what man's activity can bring about. It has accomplished wonders far surpassing Egyptian pyramids, Roman aqueducts, and Gothic cathedrals; it has conducted expeditions that put in the shade all former Exoduses of nations and crusades.

The bourgeoisie cannot exist without constantly revolutionising the instruments of production, and thereby the relations of production, and with them the whole relations of society. Conservation of the old modes of production in unaltered form, was, on the contrary, the first condition of existence for all earlier industrial classes. Constant revolutionising of production, uninterrupted disturbance of all social conditions, everlasting uncertainty and agitation distinguish the bourgeois epoch from all earlier ones. All fixed, fast-frozen relations, with their train of ancient and venerable prejudices and opinions, are swept away, all new-formed ones become antiquated before they can ossify. All that is solid melts into air, all that is holy is profaned, and man is at last compelled to face with sober senses his real conditions of life, and his relations with his kind.

The need of a constantly expanding market for its products chases the bourgeoisie over the entire surface of the globe. It must nestle everywhere, settle everywhere, establish connexions everywhere.

The bourgeoisie has through its exploitation of the world market given a cosmopolitan character to production and consumption in every country. To the great chagrin of Reactionists, it has drawn from under the feet of industry the national ground on which it stood. All old-established national industries have been destroyed or are daily being destroyed. They are dislodged by new industries, whose introduction becomes a life and death question for all civilised nations, by industries that no longer work up indigenous raw material, but raw material drawn from the remotest zones; industries whose products are consumed, not only at home, but in every quarter of the globe. In place of the old wants, satisfied by the production of the country, we find new wants, requiring for their satisfaction the products of distant lands and climes. In place of the old local and national seclusion and self-sufficiency, we have intercourse in every direction, universal inter-dependence of nations. And as in material, so also in intellectual production. The intellectual creations of individual nations become common property. National one-sidedness and narrow-mindedness become more and more impossible, and from the numerous national and local literatures, there arises a world literature.

The bourgeoisie, by the rapid improvement of all instruments of production, by the immensely facilitated means of communication, draws all, even the most barbarian, nations into civilisation. The cheap prices of commodities are the heavy artillery with which it batters down all Chinese walls, with which it forces the barbarians' intensely obstinate hatred of foreigners to capitulate. It compels all nations, on pain of extinction, to adopt the bourgeois mode of production; it compels them to introduce what it calls civilisation into their midst, i.e., to become bourgeois themselves. In one word, it creates a world after its own image.

The bourgeoisie has subjected the country to the rule of the towns. It has created enormous cities, has greatly increased the urban population as compared with the rural, and has thus rescued a considerable part of the population from the idiocy of rural life. Just as it has made the country dependent on the towns, so it has made barbarian and semi-barbarian countries dependent on the civilised ones, nations of peasants on nations of bourgeois, the East on the West.

The bourgeoisie keeps more and more doing away with the scattered state of the population, of the means of production, and of property. It has agglomerated population, centralised the means of production, and has concentrated property in a few hands. The necessary consequence of this was political centralisation. Independent, or but loosely connected provinces, with separate interests, laws, governments, and systems of taxation, became lumped together into one nation, with one government, one code of laws, one national class-interest, one frontier, and one customs-tariff.

The bourgeoisie, during its rule of scarce one hundred years, has created more massive and more colossal productive forces than have all preceding generations together. Subjection of Nature's forces to man, machinery, application of chemistry to industry and agriculture, steam-navigation, railways, electric telegraphs, clearing of whole continents for cultivation, canalisation of rivers, whole populations conjured out of the ground — what earlier century had even a presentiment that such productive forces slumbered in the lap of social labour?

We see then: the means of production and of exchange, on whose foundation the bourgeoisie built itself up, were generated in feudal society. At a certain stage in the development of these means of production and of exchange, the conditions under which feudal society produced and exchanged, the feudal organisation of agriculture and manufacturing industry, in one word, the feudal relations of property became no longer compatible with the already developed productive forces; they became so many fetters. They had to be burst asunder; they were burst asunder.

Into their place stepped free competition, accompanied by a social and political constitution adapted in it, and the economic and political sway of the bourgeois class.

A similar movement is going on before our own eyes. Modern bourgeois society, with its relations of production, of exchange and of property, a society that has conjured up such gigantic means of production and of exchange, is like the sorcerer who is no longer able to control the powers of the nether world whom he has called up by his spells. For many a decade past the history of industry and commerce is but the history of the revolt of modern productive forces against modern conditions of production, against the property relations that are the conditions for the existence of the bourgeois and of its rule. It is enough to mention the commercial crises that by their periodical return put the existence of the entire bourgeois society on its trial, each time more threateningly. In these crises, a great part not only of the existing products, but also of the previously created productive forces, are periodically destroyed. In these crises, there breaks out an epidemic that, in all earlier epochs, would have seemed an absurdity — the epidemic of over-production. Society suddenly finds itself put back into a state of momentary barbarism; it appears as if a famine, a universal war of devastation, had cut off the supply of every means of subsistence; industry and commerce seem to be destroyed; and why? Because there is too much civilisation, too much means of subsistence, too much industry, too much commerce. The productive forces at the disposal of society no longer tend to further the development of the conditions of bourgeois property; on the contrary, they have become too powerful for these conditions, by which they are fettered, and so soon as they overcome these fetters, they bring disorder into the whole of bourgeois society, endanger the existence of bourgeois property. The conditions of bourgeois society are too narrow to comprise the wealth created by them. And how does the bourgeoisie get over these crises? On the one hand by enforced destruction of a mass of productive forces; on the other, by the conquest of new markets, and by the more thorough exploitation of the old ones. That is to say, by paving the way for more extensive and more destructive crises, and by diminishing the means whereby crises are prevented.

The weapons with which the bourgeoisie felled feudalism to the ground are now turned against the bourgeoisie itself.

But not only has the bourgeoisie forged the weapons that bring death to itself; it has also called into existence the men who are to wield those weapons — the modern working class — the proletarians.

In proportion as the bourgeoisie, i.e., capital, is developed, in the same proportion is the proletariat, the modern working class, developed — a class of labourers, who live only so long as they find work, and who find work only so long as their labour increases capital. These labourers, who must sell themselves piecemeal, are a commodity, like every other article of commerce, and are consequently exposed to all the vicissitudes of competition, to all the fluctuations of the market.

Owing to the extensive use of machinery, and to the division of labour, the work of the proletarians has lost all individual character, and, consequently, all charm for the workman. He becomes an appendage of the machine, and it is only the most simple, most monotonous, and most easily acquired knack, that is required of him. Hence, the cost of production of a workman is restricted, almost entirely, to the means of subsistence that he requires for maintenance, and for the propagation of his race. But the price of a commodity, and therefore also of labour, is equal to its cost of production. In proportion, therefore, as the repulsiveness of the work increases, the wage decreases. Nay more, in proportion as the use of machinery and division of labour increases, in the same proportion the burden of toil also increases, whether by prolongation of the working hours, by the increase of the work exacted in a given time or by increased speed of machinery, etc.

Modern Industry has converted the little workshop of the patriarchal master into the great factory of the industrial capitalist. Masses of labourers, crowded into the factory, are organised like soldiers. As privates of the industrial army they are placed under the command of a perfect hierarchy of officers and sergeants. Not only are they slaves of the bourgeois class, and of the bourgeois State; they are daily and hourly enslaved by the machine, by the overlooker, and, above all, by the individual bourgeois manufacturer himself. The more openly this despotism proclaims gain to be its end and aim, the more petty, the more hateful and the more embittering it is.

The less the skill and exertion of strength implied in manual labour, in other words, the more modern industry becomes developed, the more is the labour of men superseded by that of women. Differences of age and sex have no longer any distinctive social validity for the working class. All are instruments of labour, more or less expensive to use, according to their age and sex.

No sooner is the exploitation of the labourer by the manufacturer, so far, at an end, that he receives his wages in cash, than he is set upon by the other portions of the bourgeoisie, the landlord, the shopkeeper, the pawnbroker, etc.

The lower strata of the middle class — the small tradespeople, shopkeepers, and retired tradesmen generally, the handicraftsmen and peasants — all these sink gradually into the proletariat, partly because their diminutive capital does not suffice for the scale on which Modern Industry is carried on, and is swamped in the competition with the large capitalists, partly because their specialised skill is rendered worthless by new methods of production. Thus the proletariat is recruited from all classes of the population.

The proletariat goes through various stages of development. With its birth begins its struggle with the bourgeoisie. At first the contest is carried on by individual labourers, then by the workpeople of a factory, then by the operative of one trade, in one locality, against the individual bourgeois who directly exploits them. They direct their attacks not against the bourgeois conditions of production, but against the instruments of production themselves; they destroy imported wares that compete with their labour, they smash to pieces machinery, they set factories ablaze, they seek to restore by force the vanished status of the workman of the Middle Ages.

At this stage, the labourers still form an incoherent mass scattered over the whole country, and broken up by their mutual competition. If anywhere they unite to form more compact bodies, this is not yet the consequence of their own active union, but of the union of the bourgeoisie, which class, in order to attain its own political ends, is compelled to set the whole proletariat in motion, and is moreover yet, for a time, able to do so. At this stage, therefore, the proletarians do not fight their enemies, but the enemies of their enemies, the remnants of absolute monarchy, the landowners, the non-industrial bourgeois, the petty bourgeois. Thus, the whole historical movement is concentrated in the hands of the bourgeoisie; every victory so obtained is a victory for the bourgeoisie.

But with the development of industry, the proletariat not only increases in number; it becomes concentrated in greater masses, its strength grows, and it feels that strength more. The various interests and conditions of life within the ranks of the proletariat are more and more equalised, in proportion as machinery obliterates all distinctions of labour, and nearly everywhere reduces wages to the same low level. The growing competition among the bourgeois, and the resulting commercial crises, make the wages of the workers ever more fluctuating. The increasing improvement of machinery, ever more rapidly developing, makes their livelihood more and more precarious; the collisions between individual workmen and individual bourgeois take more and more the character of collisions between two classes. Thereupon, the workers begin to form combinations (Trades' Unions) against the bourgeois; they club together in order to keep up the rate of wages; they found permanent associations in order to make provision beforehand for these occasional revolts. Here and there, the contest breaks out into riots.

Now and then the workers are victorious, but only for a time. The real fruit of their battles lies, not in the immediate result, but in the ever expanding union of the workers. This union is helped on by the improved means of communication that are created by modern industry, and that place the workers of different localities in contact with one another. It was just this contact that was needed to centralise the numerous local struggles, all of the same character, into one national struggle between classes. But every class struggle is a political struggle. And that union, to attain which the burghers of the Middle Ages, with their miserable highways, required centuries, the modern proletarian, thanks to railways, achieve in a few years.

This organisation of the proletarians into a class, and, consequently into a political party, is continually being upset again by the competition between the workers themselves. But it ever rises up again, stronger, firmer, mightier. It compels legislative recognition of particular interests of the workers, by taking advantage of the divisions among the bourgeoisie itself. Thus, the ten-hours' bill in England was carried.

Altogether collisions between the classes of the old society further, in many ways, the course of development of the proletariat. The bourgeoisie finds itself involved in a constant battle. At first with the aristocracy; later on, with those portions of the bourgeoisie itself, whose interests have become antagonistic to the progress of industry; at all time with the bourgeoisie of foreign countries. In all these battles, it sees itself compelled to appeal to the proletariat, to ask for help, and thus, to drag it into the political arena. The bourgeoisie itself, therefore, supplies the proletariat with its own elements of political and general education, in other words, it furnishes the proletariat with weapons for fighting the bourgeoisie.

Further, as we have already seen, entire sections of the ruling class are, by the advance of industry, precipitated into the proletariat, or are at least threatened in their conditions of existence. These also supply the proletariat with fresh elements of enlightenment and progress.

Finally, in times when the class struggle nears the decisive hour, the progress of dissolution going on within the ruling class, in fact within the whole range of old society, assumes such a violent, glaring character, that a small section of the ruling class cuts itself adrift, and joins the revolutionary class, the class that holds the future in its hands. Just as, therefore, at an earlier period, a section of the nobility went over to the bourgeoisie, so now a portion of the bourgeoisie goes over to the proletariat, and in particular, a portion of the bourgeois ideologists, who have raised themselves to the level of comprehending theoretically the historical movement as a whole.

Of all the classes that stand face to face with the bourgeoisie today, the proletariat alone is a really revolutionary class. The other classes decay and finally disappear in the face of Modern Industry; the proletariat is its special and essential product.

The lower middle class, the small manufacturer, the shopkeeper, the artisan, the peasant, all these fight against the bourgeoisie, to save from extinction their existence as fractions of the middle class. They are therefore not revolutionary, but conservative. Nay more, they are reactionary, for they try to roll back the wheel of history. If by chance, they are revolutionary, they are only so in view of their impending transfer into the proletariat; they thus defend not their present, but their future interests, they desert their own standpoint to place themselves at that of the proletariat.

The "dangerous class", [lumpenproletariat] the social scum, that passively rotting mass thrown off by the lowest layers of the old society, may, here and there, be swept into the movement by a proletarian revolution; its conditions of life, however, prepare it far more for the part of a bribed tool of reactionary intrigue.

In the condition of the proletariat, those of old society at large are already virtually swamped. The proletarian is without property; his relation to his wife and children has no longer anything in common with the bourgeois family relations; modern industry labour, modern subjection to capital, the same in England as in France, in America as in Germany, has stripped him of every trace of national character. Law, morality, religion, are to him so many bourgeois prejudices, behind which lurk in ambush just as many bourgeois interests.

All the preceding classes that got the upper hand sought to fortify their already acquired status by subjecting society at large to their conditions of appropriation. The proletarians cannot become masters of the productive forces of society, except by abolishing their own previous mode of appropriation, and thereby also every other previous mode of appropriation. They have nothing of their own to secure and to fortify; their mission is to destroy all previous securities for, and insurances of, individual property.

All previous historical movements were movements of minorities, or in the interest of minorities. The proletarian movement is the self-conscious, independent movement of the immense majority, in the interest of the immense majority. The proletariat, the lowest stratum of our present society, cannot stir, cannot raise itself up, without the whole superincumbent strata of official society being sprung into the air.

Though not in substance, yet in form, the struggle of the proletariat with the bourgeoisie is at first a national struggle. The proletariat of each country must, of course, first of all settle matters with its own bourgeoisie.

In depicting the most general phases of the development of the proletariat, we traced the more or less veiled civil war, raging within existing society, up to the point where that war breaks out into open revolution, and where the violent overthrow of the bourgeoisie lays the foundation for the sway of the proletariat.

Hitherto, every form of society has been based, as we have already seen, on the antagonism of oppressing and oppressed classes. But in order to oppress a class, certain conditions must be assured to it under which it can, at least, continue its slavish existence. The serf, in the period of serfdom, raised himself to membership in the commune, just as the petty bourgeois, under the yoke of the feudal absolutism, managed to develop into a bourgeois. The modern labourer, on the contrary, instead of rising with the process of industry, sinks deeper and deeper below the conditions of existence of his own class. He becomes a pauper, and pauperism develops more rapidly than population and wealth. And here it becomes evident, that the bourgeoisie is unfit any longer to be the ruling class in society, and to impose its conditions of existence upon society as an over-riding law. It is unfit to rule because it is incompetent to assure an existence to its slave within his slavery, because it cannot help letting him sink into such a state, that it has to feed him, instead of being fed by him. Society can no longer live under this bourgeoisie, in other words, its existence is no longer compatible with society.

The essential conditions for the existence and for the sway of the bourgeois class is the formation and augmentation of capital; the condition for capital is wage-labour. Wage-labour rests exclusively on competition between the labourers. The advance of industry, whose involuntary promoter is the bourgeoisie, replaces the isolation of the labourers, due to competition, by the revolutionary combination, due to association. The development of Modern Industry, therefore, cuts from under its feet the very foundation on which the bourgeoisie produces and appropriates products. What the bourgeoisie therefore produces, above all, are its own grave-diggers. Its fall and the victory of the proletariat are equally inevitable.

In what relation do the Communists stand to the proletarians as a whole?

The Communists do not form a separate party opposed to the other working-class parties.

They have no interests separate and apart from those of the proletariat as a whole.

They do not set up any sectarian principles of their own, by which to shape and mould the proletarian movement.

The Communists are distinguished from the other working-class parties by this only: 1. In the national struggles of the proletarians of the different countries, they point out and bring to the front the common interests of the entire proletariat, independently of all nationality. 2. In the various stages of development which the struggle of the working class against the bourgeoisie has to pass through, they always and everywhere represent the interests of the movement as a whole.

The Communists, therefore, are on the one hand, practically, the most advanced and resolute section of the working-class parties of every country, that section which pushes forward all others; on the other hand, theoretically, they have over the great mass of the proletariat the advantage of clearly understanding the line of march, the conditions, and the ultimate general results of the proletarian movement.

The immediate aim of the Communists is the same as that of all other proletarian parties: formation of the proletariat into a class, overthrow of the bourgeois supremacy, conquest of political power by the proletariat.

The theoretical conclusions of the Communists are in no way based on ideas or principles that have been invented, or discovered, by this or that would-be universal reformer.

They merely express, in general terms, actual relations springing from an existing class struggle, from a historical movement going on under our very eyes. The abolition of existing property relations is not at all a distinctive feature of communism.

All property relations in the past have continually been subject to historical change consequent upon the change in historical conditions.

The French Revolution, for example, abolished feudal property in favour of bourgeois property.

The distinguishing feature of Communism is not the abolition of property generally, but the abolition of bourgeois property. But modern bourgeois private property is the final and most complete expression of the system of producing and appropriating products, that is based on class antagonisms, on the exploitation of the many by the few.

In this sense, the theory of the Communists may be summed up in the single sentence: Abolition of private property.

We Communists have been reproached with the desire of abolishing the right of personally acquiring property as the fruit of a man's own labour, which property is alleged to be the groundwork of all personal freedom, activity and independence.

Hard-won, self-acquired, self-earned property! Do you mean the property of petty artisan and of the small peasant, a form of property that preceded the bourgeois form? There is no need to abolish that; the development of industry has to a great extent already destroyed it, and is still destroying it daily.

Or do you mean the modern bourgeois private property?

But does wage-labour create any property for the labourer? Not a bit. It creates capital, i.e., that kind of property which exploits wage-labour, and which cannot increase except upon condition of begetting a new supply of wage-labour for fresh exploitation. Property, in its present form, is based on the antagonism of capital and wage labour. Let us examine both sides of this antagonism.

To be a capitalist, is to have not only a purely personal, but a social status in production. Capital is a collective product, and only by the united action of many members, nay, in the last resort, only by the united action of all members of society, can it be set in motion.

Capital is therefore not only personal; it is a social power.

When, therefore, capital is converted into common property, into the property of all members of society, personal property is not thereby transformed into social property. It is only the social character of the property that is changed. It loses its class character.

Let us now take wage-labour.

The average price of wage-labour is the minimum wage, i.e., that quantum of the means of subsistence which is absolutely requisite to keep the labourer in bare existence as a labourer. What, therefore, the wage-labourer appropriates by means of his labour, merely suffices to prolong and reproduce a bare existence. We by no means intend to abolish this personal appropriation of the products of labour, an appropriation that is made for the maintenance and reproduction of human life, and that leaves no surplus wherewith to command the labour of others. All that we want to do away with is the miserable character of this appropriation, under which the labourer lives merely to increase capital, and is allowed to live only in so far as the interest of the ruling class requires it.

In bourgeois society, living labour is but a means to increase accumulated labour. In Communist society, accumulated labour is but a means to widen, to enrich, to promote the existence of the labourer.

In bourgeois society, therefore, the past dominates the present; in Communist society, the present dominates the past. In bourgeois society capital is independent and has individuality, while the living person is dependent and has no individuality.

And the abolition of this state of things is called by the bourgeois, abolition of individuality and freedom! And rightly so. The abolition of bourgeois individuality, bourgeois independence, and bourgeois freedom is undoubtedly aimed at.

By freedom is meant, under the present bourgeois conditions of production, free trade, free selling and buying.

But if selling and buying disappears, free selling and buying disappears also. This talk about free selling and buying, and all the other "brave words" of our bourgeois about freedom in general, have a meaning, if any, only in contrast with restricted selling and buying, with the fettered traders of the Middle Ages, but have no meaning when opposed to the Communistic abolition of buying and selling, of the bourgeois conditions of production, and of the bourgeoisie itself.

You are horrified at our intending to do away with private property. But in your existing society, private property is already done away with for nine-tenths of the population; its existence for the few is solely due to its non-existence in the hands of those nine-tenths. You reproach us, therefore, with intending to do away with a form of property, the necessary condition for whose existence is the non-existence of any property for the immense majority of society.

In one word, you reproach us with intending to do away with your property. Precisely so; that is just what we intend.

From the moment when labour can no longer be converted into capital, money, or rent, into a social power capable of being monopolised, i.e., from the moment when individual property can no longer be transformed into bourgeois property, into capital, from that moment, you say, individuality vanishes.

You must, therefore, confess that by "individual" you mean no other person than the bourgeois, than the middle-class owner of property. This person must, indeed, be swept out of the way, and made impossible.

Communism deprives no man of the power to appropriate the products of society; all that it does is to deprive him of the power to subjugate the labour of others by means of such appropriations.

It has been objected that upon the abolition of private property, all work will cease, and universal laziness will overtake us.

According to this, bourgeois society ought long ago to have gone to the dogs through sheer idleness; for those of its members who work, acquire nothing, and those who acquire anything do not work. The whole of this objection is but another expression of the tautology: that there can no longer be any wage-labour when there is no longer any capital.

All objections urged against the Communistic mode of producing and appropriating material products, have, in the same way, been urged against the Communistic mode of producing and appropriating intellectual products. Just as, to the bourgeois, the disappearance of class property is the disappearance of production itself, so the disappearance of class culture is to him identical with the disappearance of all culture.

That culture, the loss of which he laments, is, for the enormous majority, a mere training to act as a machine.

But don't wrangle with us so long as you apply, to our intended abolition of bourgeois property, the standard of your bourgeois notions of freedom, culture, law, &c. Your very ideas are but the outgrowth of the conditions of your bourgeois production and bourgeois property, just as your jurisprudence is but the will of your class made into a law for all, a will whose essential character and direction are determined by the economical conditions of existence of your class.

The selfish misconception that induces you to transform into eternal laws of nature and of reason, the social forms springing from your present mode of production and form of property – historical relations that rise and disappear in the progress of production – this misconception you share with every ruling class that has preceded you. What you see clearly in the case of ancient property, what you admit in the case of feudal property, you are of course forbidden to admit in the case of your own bourgeois form of property.

Abolition [Aufhebung] of the family! Even the most radical flare up at this infamous proposal of the Communists.

On what foundation is the present family, the bourgeois family, based? On capital, on private gain. In its completely developed form, this family exists only among the bourgeoisie. But this state of things finds its complement in the practical absence of the family among the proletarians, and in public prostitution.

The bourgeois family will vanish as a matter of course when its complement vanishes, and both will vanish with the vanishing of capital.

Do you charge us with wanting to stop the exploitation of children by their parents? To this crime we plead guilty.

But, you say, we destroy the most hallowed of relations, when we replace home education by social.

And your education! Is not that also social, and determined by the social conditions under which you educate, by the intervention direct or indirect, of society, by means of schools, &c.? The Communists have not invented the intervention of society in education; they do but seek to alter the character of that intervention, and to rescue education from the influence of the ruling class.

The bourgeois clap-trap about the family and education, about the hallowed co-relation of parents and child, becomes all the more disgusting, the more, by the action of Modern Industry, all the family ties among the proletarians are torn asunder, and their children transformed into simple articles of commerce and instruments of labour.

But you Communists would introduce community of women, screams the bourgeoisie in chorus.

The bourgeois sees his wife a mere instrument of production. He hears that the instruments of production are to be exploited in common, and, naturally, can come to no other conclusion that the lot of being common to all will likewise fall to the women.

He has not even a suspicion that the real point aimed at is to do away with the status of women as mere instruments of production.

For the rest, nothing is more ridiculous than the virtuous indignation of our bourgeois at the community of women which, they pretend, is to be openly and officially established by the Communists. The Communists have no need to introduce community of women; it has existed almost from time immemorial.

Our bourgeois, not content with having wives and daughters of their proletarians at their disposal, not to speak of common prostitutes, take the greatest pleasure in seducing each other's wives.

Bourgeois marriage is, in reality, a system of wives in common and thus, at the most, what the Communists might possibly be reproached with is that they desire to introduce, in substitution for a hypocritically concealed, an openly legalised community of women. For the rest, it is self-evident that the abolition of the present system of production must bring with it the abolition of the community of women springing from that system, i.e., of prostitution both public and private.

The Communists are further reproached with desiring to abolish countries and nationality.

The working men have no country. We cannot take from them what they have not got. Since the proletariat must first of all acquire political supremacy, must rise to be the leading class of the nation, must constitute itself the nation, it is so far, itself national, though not in the bourgeois sense of the word.

National differences and antagonism between peoples are daily more and more vanishing, owing to the development of the bourgeoisie, to freedom of commerce, to the world market, to uniformity in the mode of production and in the conditions of life corresponding thereto.

The supremacy of the proletariat will cause them to vanish still faster. United action, of the leading civilised countries at least, is one of the first conditions for the emancipation of the proletariat.

In proportion as the exploitation of one individual by another will also be put an end to, the exploitation of one nation by another will also be put an end to. In proportion as the antagonism between classes within the nation vanishes, the hostility of one nation to another will come to an end.

The charges against Communism made from a religious, a philosophical and, generally, from an ideological standpoint, are not deserving of serious examination.

Does it require deep intuition to comprehend that man's ideas, views, and conception, in one word, man's consciousness, changes with every change in the conditions of his material existence, in his social relations and in his social life?

What else does the history of ideas prove, than that intellectual production changes its character in proportion as material production is changed? The ruling ideas of each age have ever been the ideas of its ruling class.

When people speak of the ideas that revolutionise society, they do but express that fact that within the old society the elements of a new one have been created, and that the dissolution of the old ideas keeps even pace with the dissolution of the old conditions of existence.

When the ancient world was in its last throes, the ancient religions were overcome by Christianity. When Christian ideas succumbed in the 18th century to rationalist ideas, feudal society fought its death battle with the then revolutionary bourgeoisie. The ideas of religious liberty and freedom of conscience merely gave expression to the sway of free competition within the domain of knowledge.

"Undoubtedly," it will be said, "religious, moral, philosophical, and juridical ideas have been modified in the course of historical development. But religion, morality, philosophy, political science, and law, constantly survived this change."

"There are, besides, eternal truths, such as Freedom, Justice, etc., that are common to all states of society. But Communism abolishes eternal truths, it abolishes all religion, and all morality, instead of constituting them on a new basis; it therefore acts in contradiction to all past historical experience."

What does this accusation reduce itself to? The history of all past society has consisted in the development of class antagonisms, antagonisms that assumed different forms at different epochs.

But whatever form they may have taken, one fact is common to all past ages, viz., the exploitation of one part of society by the other. No wonder, then, that the social consciousness of past ages, despite all the multiplicity and variety it displays, moves within certain common forms, or general ideas, which cannot completely vanish except with the total disappearance of class antagonisms.

The Communist revolution is the most radical rupture with traditional property relations; no wonder that its development involved the most radical rupture with traditional ideas.

But let us have done with the bourgeois objections to Communism.

We have seen above, that the first step in the revolution by the working class is to raise the proletariat to the position of ruling class to win the battle of democracy.

The proletariat will use its political supremacy to wrest, by degree, all capital from the bourgeoisie, to centralise all instruments of production in the hands of the State, i.e., of the proletariat organised as the ruling class; and to increase the total productive forces as rapidly as possible.

Of course, in the beginning, this cannot be effected except by means of despotic inroads on the rights of property, and on the conditions of bourgeois production; by means of measures, therefore, which appear economically insufficient and untenable, but which, in the course of the movement, outstrip themselves, necessitate further inroads upon the old social order, and are unavoidable as a means of entirely revolutionising the mode of production.

These measures will, of course, be different in different countries.

Nevertheless, in most advanced countries, the following will be pretty generally applicable.

1. Abolition of property in land and application of all rents of land to public purposes.
2. A heavy progressive or graduated income tax.
3. Abolition of all rights of inheritance.
4. Confiscation of the property of all emigrants and rebels.
5. Centralisation of credit in the hands of the state, by means of a national bank with State capital and an exclusive monopoly.
6. Centralisation of the means of communication and transport in the hands of the State.
7. Extension of factories and instruments of production owned by the State; the bringing into cultivation of waste-lands, and the improvement of the soil generally in accordance with a common plan.
8. Equal liability of all to work. Establishment of industrial armies, especially for agriculture.
9. Combination of agriculture with manufacturing industries; gradual abolition of all the distinction between town and country by a more equable distribution of the populace over the country.
10. Free education for all children in public schools. Abolition of

children's factory labour in its present form. Combination of education with industrial production, &c, &c.

When, in the course of development, class distinctions have disappeared, and all production has been concentrated in the hands of a vast association of the whole nation, the public power will lose its political character. Political power, properly so called, is merely the organised power of one class for oppressing another. If the proletariat during its contest with the bourgeoisie is compelled, by the force of circumstances, to organise itself as a class, if, by means of a revolution, it makes itself the ruling class, and, as such, sweeps away by force the old conditions of production, then it will, along with these conditions, have swept away the conditions for the existence of class antagonisms and of classes generally, and will thereby have abolished its own supremacy as a class.

In place of the old bourgeois society, with its classes and class antagonisms, we shall have an association, in which the free development of each is the condition for the free development of all.

# 1. Reactionary Socialism

### *A. Feudal Socialism*

Owing to their historical position, it became the vocation of the aristocracies of France and England to write pamphlets against modern bourgeois society. In the French Revolution of July 1830, and in the English reform agitation[i], these aristocracies again succumbed to the hateful upstart. Thenceforth, a serious political struggle was altogether out of the question. A literary battle alone remained possible. But even in the domain of literature the old cries of the restoration period had become impossible.[5]

In order to arouse sympathy, the aristocracy was obliged to lose sight, apparently, of its own interests, and to formulate their indictment against the bourgeoisie in the interest of the exploited working class alone. Thus, the aristocracy took their revenge by singing lampoons on their new masters and whispering in his ears sinister prophesies of coming catastrophe.

In this way arose feudal Socialism: half lamentation, half lampoon; half an echo of the past, half menace of the future; at times, by its bitter, witty and incisive criticism, striking the bourgeoisie to the very heart's core; but always ludicrous in its

---

[5] Not the English Restoration (1660-1689), but the French Restoration (1814-1830). [Note by Engels to the English edition of 1888.]

effect, through total incapacity to comprehend the march of modern history.

The aristocracy, in order to rally the people to them, waved the proletarian alms-bag in front for a banner. But the people, so often as it joined them, saw on their hindquarters the old feudal coats of arms, and deserted with loud and irreverent laughter.

One section of the French Legitimists and "Young England" exhibited this spectacle.

In pointing out that their mode of exploitation was different to that of the bourgeoisie, the feudalists forget that they exploited under circumstances and conditions that were quite different and that are now antiquated. In showing that, under their rule, the modern proletariat never existed, they forget that the modern bourgeoisie is the necessary offspring of their own form of society.

For the rest, so little do they conceal the reactionary character of their criticism that their chief accusation against the bourgeois amounts to this, that under the bourgeois régime a class is being developed which is destined to cut up root and branch the old order of society.

What they upbraid the bourgeoisie with is not so much that it creates a proletariat as that it creates a revolutionary proletariat.

In political practice, therefore, they join in all coercive measures against the working class; and in ordinary life, despite their high-falutin phrases, they stoop to pick up the golden apples dropped from the tree of industry, and to barter truth, love, and honour, for traffic in wool, beetroot-sugar, and potato spirits.[6]

---

[6] This applies chiefly to Germany, where the landed aristocracy and squirearchy have large portions of their estates cultivated for their

As the parson has ever gone hand in hand with the landlord, so has Clerical Socialism with Feudal Socialism.

Nothing is easier than to give Christian asceticism a Socialist tinge. Has not Christianity declaimed against private property, against marriage, against the State? Has it not preached in the place of these, charity and poverty, celibacy and mortification of the flesh, monastic life and Mother Church? Christian Socialism is but the holy water with which the priest consecrates the heart-burnings of the aristocrat.


## B. Petty-Bourgeois Socialism

The feudal aristocracy was not the only class that was ruined by the bourgeoisie, not the only class whose conditions of existence pined and perished in the atmosphere of modern bourgeois society. The medieval burgesses and the small peasant proprietors were the precursors of the modern bourgeoisie. In those countries which are but little developed, industrially and commercially, these two classes still vegetate side by side with the rising bourgeoisie.

In countries where modern civilisation has become fully developed, a new class of petty bourgeois has been formed, fluctuating between proletariat and bourgeoisie, and ever renewing itself as a supplementary part of bourgeois society. The individual members of this class, however, are being constantly hurled down into the proletariat by the action of competition, and, as modern industry develops, they even see

---

own account by stewards, and are, moreover, extensive beetroot-sugar manufacturers and distillers of potato spirits. The wealthier British aristocracy are, as yet, rather above that; but they, too, know how to make up for declining rents by lending their names to floaters or more or less shady joint-stock companies. [Note by Engels to the English edition of 1888.]

the moment approaching when they will completely disappear as an independent section of modern society, to be replaced in manufactures, agriculture and commerce, by overlookers, bailiffs and shopmen.

In countries like France, where the peasants constitute far more than half of the population, it was natural that writers who sided with the proletariat against the bourgeoisie should use, in their criticism of the bourgeois régime, the standard of the peasant and petty bourgeois, and from the standpoint of these intermediate classes, should take up the cudgels for the working class. Thus arose petty-bourgeois Socialism. Sismondi was the head of this school, not only in France but also in England.

This school of Socialism dissected with great acuteness the contradictions in the conditions of modern production. It laid bare the hypocritical apologies of economists. It proved, incontrovertibly, the disastrous effects of machinery and division of labour; the concentration of capital and land in a few hands; overproduction and crises; it pointed out the inevitable ruin of the petty bourgeois and peasant, the misery of the proletariat, the anarchy in production, the crying inequalities in the distribution of wealth, the industrial war of extermination between nations, the dissolution of old moral bonds, of the old family relations, of the old nationalities.

In its positive aims, however, this form of Socialism aspires either to restoring the old means of production and of exchange, and with them the old property relations, and the old society, or to cramping the modern means of production and of exchange within the framework of the old property relations that have been, and were bound to be, exploded by those means. In either case, it is both reactionary and Utopian.

Its last words are: corporate guilds for manufacture; patriarchal relations in agriculture.

Ultimately, when stubborn historical facts had dispersed all intoxicating effects of self-deception, this form of Socialism ended in a miserable fit of the blues.


## C. German or "True" Socialism

The Socialist and Communist literature of France, a literature that originated under the pressure of a bourgeoisie in power, and that was the expressions of the struggle against this power, was introduced into Germany at a time when the bourgeoisie, in that country, had just begun its contest with feudal absolutism.

German philosophers, would-be philosophers, and beaux esprits (men of letters), eagerly seized on this literature, only forgetting, that when these writings immigrated from France into Germany, French social conditions had not immigrated along with them. In contact with German social conditions, this French literature lost all its immediate practical significance and assumed a purely literary aspect. Thus, to the German philosophers of the Eighteenth Century, the demands of the first French Revolution were nothing more than the demands of "Practical Reason" in general, and the utterance of the will of the revolutionary French bourgeoisie signified, in their eyes, the laws of pure Will, of Will as it was bound to be, of true human Will generally.

The work of the German literati consisted solely in bringing the new French ideas into harmony with their ancient philosophical conscience, or rather, in annexing the French ideas without deserting their own philosophic point of view.

This annexation took place in the same way in which a foreign language is appropriated, namely, by translation.

It is well known how the monks wrote silly lives of Catholic Saints over the manuscripts on which the classical works of ancient heathendom had been written. The German literati reversed this process with the profane French literature. They wrote their philosophical nonsense beneath the French original. For instance, beneath the French criticism of the economic functions of money, they wrote "Alienation of Humanity", and beneath the French criticism of the bourgeois state they wrote "Dethronement of the Category of the General", and so forth.

The introduction of these philosophical phrases at the back of the French historical criticisms, they dubbed "Philosophy of Action", "True Socialism", "German Science of Socialism", "Philosophical Foundation of Socialism", and so on.

The French Socialist and Communist literature was thus completely emasculated. And, since it ceased in the hands of the German to express the struggle of one class with the other, he felt conscious of having overcome "French one-sidedness" and of representing, not true requirements, but the requirements of Truth; not the interests of the proletariat, but the interests of Human Nature, of Man in general, who belongs to no class, has no reality, who exists only in the misty realm of philosophical fantasy.

This German socialism, which took its schoolboy task so seriously and solemnly, and extolled its poor stock-in-trade in such a mountebank fashion, meanwhile gradually lost its pedantic innocence.

The fight of the Germans, and especially of the Prussian bourgeoisie, against feudal aristocracy and absolute monarchy, in other words, the liberal movement, became more earnest.

By this, the long-wished for opportunity was offered to "True" Socialism of confronting the political movement with the

Socialist demands, of hurling the traditional anathemas against liberalism, against representative government, against bourgeois competition, bourgeois freedom of the press, bourgeois legislation, bourgeois liberty and equality, and of preaching to the masses that they had nothing to gain, and everything to lose, by this bourgeois movement. German Socialism forgot, in the nick of time, that the French criticism, whose silly echo it was, presupposed the existence of modern bourgeois society, with its corresponding economic conditions of existence, and the political constitution adapted thereto, the very things those attainment was the object of the pending struggle in Germany.

To the absolute governments, with their following of parsons, professors, country squires, and officials, it served as a welcome scarecrow against the threatening bourgeoisie.

It was a sweet finish, after the bitter pills of flogging and bullets, with which these same governments, just at that time, dosed the German working-class risings.

While this "True" Socialism thus served the government as a weapon for fighting the German bourgeoisie, it, at the same time, directly represented a reactionary interest, the interest of German Philistines. In Germany, the petty-bourgeois class, a relic of the sixteenth century, and since then constantly cropping up again under the various forms, is the real social basis of the existing state of things.

To preserve this class is to preserve the existing state of things in Germany. The industrial and political supremacy of the bourgeoisie threatens it with certain destruction — on the one hand, from the concentration of capital; on the other, from the rise of a revolutionary proletariat. "True" Socialism appeared to kill these two birds with one stone. It spread like an epidemic.

The robe of speculative cobwebs, embroidered with flowers of rhetoric, steeped in the dew of sickly sentiment, this transcendental robe in which the German Socialists wrapped their sorry "eternal truths", all skin and bone, served to wonderfully increase the sale of their goods amongst such a public.

And on its part German Socialism recognised, more and more, its own calling as the bombastic representative of the petty-bourgeois Philistine.

It proclaimed the German nation to be the model nation, and the German petty Philistine to be the typical man. To every villainous meanness of this model man, it gave a hidden, higher, Socialistic interpretation, the exact contrary of its real character. It went to the extreme length of directly opposing the "brutally destructive" tendency of Communism, and of proclaiming its supreme and impartial contempt of all class struggles. With very few exceptions, all the so-called Socialist and Communist publications that now (1847) circulate in Germany belong to the domain of this foul and enervating literature.[7]

## 2. Conservative or Bourgeois Socialism

A part of the bourgeoisie is desirous of redressing social grievances in order to secure the continued existence of bourgeois society.

To this section belong economists, philanthropists, humanitarians, improvers of the condition of the working class, organisers of charity, members of societies for the prevention of

---

[7] The revolutionary storm of 1848 swept away this whole shabby tendency and cured its protagonists of the desire to dabble in socialism. The chief representative and classical type of this tendency is Mr Karl Gruen. [Note by Engels to the German edition of 1890.]

cruelty to animals, temperance fanatics, hole-and-corner reformers of every imaginable kind. This form of socialism has, moreover, been worked out into complete systems.

We may cite Proudhon's Philosophie de la Misère as an example of this form.

The Socialistic bourgeois want all the advantages of modern social conditions without the struggles and dangers necessarily resulting therefrom. They desire the existing state of society, minus its revolutionary and disintegrating elements. They wish for a bourgeoisie without a proletariat. The bourgeoisie naturally conceives the world in which it is supreme to be the best; and bourgeois Socialism develops this comfortable conception into various more or less complete systems. In requiring the proletariat to carry out such a system, and thereby to march straightway into the social New Jerusalem, it but requires in reality, that the proletariat should remain within the bounds of existing society, but should cast away all its hateful ideas concerning the bourgeoisie.

A second, and more practical, but less systematic, form of this Socialism sought to depreciate every revolutionary movement in the eyes of the working class by showing that no mere political reform, but only a change in the material conditions of existence, in economical relations, could be of any advantage to them. By changes in the material conditions of existence, this form of Socialism, however, by no means understands abolition of the bourgeois relations of production, an abolition that can be affected only by a revolution, but administrative reforms, based on the continued existence of these relations; reforms, therefore, that in no respect affect the relations between capital and labour, but, at the best, lessen the cost, and simplify the administrative work, of bourgeois government.

Bourgeois Socialism attains adequate expression when, and only when, it becomes a mere figure of speech.

Free trade: for the benefit of the working class. Protective duties: for the benefit of the working class. Prison Reform: for the benefit of the working class. This is the last word and the only seriously meant word of bourgeois socialism.

It is summed up in the phrase: the bourgeois is a bourgeois — for the benefit of the working class.

## 3. Critical-Utopian Socialism and Communism

We do not here refer to that literature which, in every great modern revolution, has always given voice to the demands of the proletariat, such as the writings of Babeuf and others.

The first direct attempts of the proletariat to attain its own ends, made in times of universal excitement, when feudal society was being overthrown, necessarily failed, owing to the then undeveloped state of the proletariat, as well as to the absence of the economic conditions for its emancipation, conditions that had yet to be produced, and could be produced by the impending bourgeois epoch alone. The revolutionary literature that accompanied these first movements of the proletariat had necessarily a reactionary character. It inculcated universal asceticism and social levelling in its crudest form.

The Socialist and Communist systems, properly so called, those of Saint-Simon, Fourier, Owen, and others, spring into existence in the early undeveloped period, described above, of the struggle between proletariat and bourgeoisie (see Section 1. Bourgeois and Proletarians).

The founders of these systems see, indeed, the class antagonisms, as well as the action of the decomposing elements in the prevailing form of society. But the proletariat, as yet in its infancy, offers to them the spectacle of a class without any historical initiative or any independent political movement.

Since the development of class antagonism keeps even pace with the development of industry, the economic situation, as they find it, does not as yet offer to them the material conditions for the emancipation of the proletariat. They therefore search after a new social science, after new social laws, that are to create these conditions.

Historical action is to yield to their personal inventive action; historically created conditions of emancipation to fantastic ones; and the gradual, spontaneous class organisation of the proletariat to an organisation of society especially contrived by these inventors. Future history resolves itself, in their eyes, into the propaganda and the practical carrying out of their social plans.

In the formation of their plans, they are conscious of caring chiefly for the interests of the working class, as being the most suffering class. Only from the point of view of being the most suffering class does the proletariat exist for them.

The undeveloped state of the class struggle, as well as their own surroundings, causes Socialists of this kind to consider themselves far superior to all class antagonisms. They want to improve the condition of every member of society, even that of the most favoured. Hence, they habitually appeal to society at large, without the distinction of class; nay, by preference, to the ruling class. For how can people, when once they understand their system, fail to see in it the best possible plan of the best possible state of society?

Hence, they reject all political, and especially all revolutionary action; they wish to attain their ends by peaceful means, necessarily doomed to failure, and by the force of example, to pave the way for the new social Gospel.

Such fantastic pictures of future society, painted at a time when the proletariat is still in a very undeveloped state and has but a fantastic conception of its own position, correspond with the first instinctive yearnings of that class for a general reconstruction of society.

But these Socialist and Communist publications contain also a critical element. They attack every principle of existing society. Hence, they are full of the most valuable materials for the enlightenment of the working class. The practical measures proposed in them — such as the abolition of the distinction between town and country, of the family, of the carrying on of industries for the account of private individuals, and of the wage system, the proclamation of social harmony, the conversion of the function of the state into a more superintendence of production — all these proposals point solely to the disappearance of class antagonisms which were, at that time, only just cropping up, and which, in these publications, are recognised in their earliest indistinct and undefined forms only. These proposals, therefore, are of a purely Utopian character.

The significance of Critical-Utopian Socialism and Communism bears an inverse relation to historical development. In proportion as the modern class struggle develops and takes definite shape, this fantastic standing apart from the contest, these fantastic attacks on it, lose all practical value and all theoretical justification. Therefore, although the originators of these systems were, in many respects, revolutionary, their disciples have, in every case, formed mere reactionary sects. They hold fast by the original views of their masters, in opposition to the progressive historical development of the proletariat. They, therefore, endeavour, and that consistently, to deaden the class struggle and to reconcile the class antagonisms. They still dream of experimental realisation of their social Utopias, of founding isolated "phalansteres", of establishing "Home Colonies", or setting up a "Little Icaria"[8] — duodecimo editions of the New Jerusalem — and to realise all these castles in the air, they are compelled to appeal to the feelings and purses of the bourgeois. By degrees, they sink into the category of the reactionary [or] conservative Socialists depicted above, differing from these only by more systematic pedantry, and by their fanatical and superstitious belief in the miraculous effects of their social science.

They, therefore, violently oppose all political action on the part of the working class; such action, according to them, can only result from blind unbelief in the new Gospel.

The Owenites in England, and the Fourierists in France, respectively, oppose the Chartists and the Réformistes.

---

[8] Phalanstéres were Socialist colonies on the plan of Charles Fourier; Icaria was the name given by Cabet to his Utopia and, later on, to his American Communist colony. [Note by Engels to the English edition of 1888.]

"Home Colonies" were what Owen called his Communist model societies. Phalanstéres was the name of the public palaces planned by Fourier. Icaria was the name given to the Utopian land of fancy, whose Communist institutions Cabet portrayed. [Note by Engels to the German edition of 1890.]

Section II has made clear the relations of the Communists to the existing working-class parties, such as the Chartists in England and the Agrarian Reformers in America.

The Communists fight for the attainment of the immediate aims, for the enforcement of the momentary interests of the working class; but in the movement of the present, they also represent and take care of the future of that movement. In France, the Communists ally with the Social-Democrats[9] against the conservative and radical bourgeoisie, reserving, however, the right to take up a critical position in regard to phases and illusions traditionally handed down from the great Revolution.

In Switzerland, they support the Radicals, without losing sight of the fact that this party consists of antagonistic elements, partly of Democratic Socialists, in the French sense, partly of radical bourgeois.

In Poland, they support the party that insists on an agrarian revolution as the prime condition for national emancipation, that party which fomented the insurrection of Cracow in 1846.

In Germany, they fight with the bourgeoisie whenever it acts in a revolutionary way, against the absolute monarchy, the feudal squirearchy, and the petty bourgeoisie.

But they never cease, for a single instant, to instill into the working class the clearest possible recognition of the hostile

---

[9] The party then represented in Parliament by Ledru-Rollin, in literature by Louis Blanc, in the daily press by the Réforme. The name of Social-Democracy signifies, with these its inventors, a section of the Democratic or Republican Party more or less tinged with socialism. [Engels, English Edition 1888]

antagonism between bourgeoisie and proletariat, in order that the German workers may straightway use, as so many weapons against the bourgeoisie, the social and political conditions that the bourgeoisie must necessarily introduce along with its supremacy, and in order that, after the fall of the reactionary classes in Germany, the fight against the bourgeoisie itself may immediately begin.

The Communists turn their attention chiefly to Germany, because that country is on the eve of a bourgeois revolution that is bound to be carried out under more advanced conditions of European civilisation and with a much more developed proletariat than that of England was in the seventeenth, and France in the eighteenth century, and because the bourgeois revolution in Germany will be but the prelude to an immediately following proletarian revolution.

In short, the Communists everywhere support every revolutionary movement against the existing social and political order of things.

In all these movements, they bring to the front, as the leading question in each, the property question, no matter what its degree of development at the time.

Finally, they labour everywhere for the union and agreement of the democratic parties of all countries.

The Communists disdain to conceal their views and aims. They openly declare that their ends can be attained only by the forcible overthrow of all existing social conditions. Let the ruling classes tremble at a Communistic revolution. The proletarians have nothing to lose but their chains. They have a world to win.

# Working Men of All Countries, Unite![ii]

## Summary

Comrade, it's time overthrow your boss! Let's take over the place ourselves and end these miserable working conditions!

Maybe subversive thoughts like those have crossed your mind while you've toiled away at work, right? Or maybe you've heard politicians accusing other politicians of being communists. Maybe you've even heard someone called a commie or a pinko or a red, but you don't know what any of it *really* means.

*The Communist Manifesto*, published in 1848, is the single document most responsible for launching the often-feared political philosophy of communism. It straight up tells you to revolt against the rich, and it tells you why you should.

Here's the gist of the *Manifesto*, fast enough for you to read before you have to wake up and slave away at your job tomorrow: Marx describes how the bourgeoisie (the rich capitalists) rose to power over the aristocracy (kings and feudal lords), how the capitalists maintain power, and how they're now confronted by the proletariat (the working poor who are paid wages), who as communists will overthrow them. Once the proletarians take charge, they're supposed to set up a vanguard state—a temporary government to transition society from capitalism to communism. This will be a system where the most important private property—the means of production (factories, agricultural land, machinery)—will be shared in common, and no one will profit to exploit others.

Yeah, it's an incredibly controversial work. A lot of people blame the *Communist Manifesto* for the fact that Soviet dictator Josef Stalin put *tens of millions of people* into Gulags, or forced labor camps, and committed all kinds of other horrors. On the other hand, some say communism has never been implemented properly—perhaps because the continued existence of rival capitalism doesn't allow it.

Authors Karl Marx and Friedrich Engels didn't win any awards for this document, but they got a bigger prize: the manifesto, which is primarily Marx's work, is famous because *it changed the world*—and still does. It inspired the leaders of the Russian Revolution to overthrow the tsarist aristocracy and set up the communist Bolshevik government that led to the communist Soviet Union, one of the most powerful countries of the 20th century. China, Cuba, and other countries consider themselves communist to this day.

All that wouldn't have happened if Marx, inspired by the bad working conditions for the workforce, hadn't written this little book.

Do you jump out of bed every weekday morning and cheer, overcome with joy that you're about to go to work or school? Maybe, but there's a good chance you hate your job or hate having to get the degree pretty much required for you to someday bring home a decent paycheck.

On the other hand, maybe on *weekend* mornings (okay, afternoons) you do jump out of bed and cheer, because the day off work or school means you have a chance to practice your guitar or improve your garden.

What's the difference between these two? Karl Marx would say that Monday through Friday, you're *alienated* from your work. The commercial product you're slaving away at for your boss, or the math busywork you're filling out to impress your future boss, isn't something you get to use in your own life according to your own values.

Instead of living on an Earth where your work-product is tied to the rest of your life, you feel like a space alien trapped on a planet where you're obeying someone else's rules so that the authorities— teachers, bosses—can profit off you. The joy of making for the sake of making is overtaken by the conditions you're stuck in if you want to make stuff at all.

Marx thinks that as a result, we slowly begin to treat each other as commodities: the person who works at the cash register becomes a cashier, and the cashier becomes an extension of the cash register. We rarely see deeply into one another, and we disappear into unfulfilling lives that boil down pretty much to money.

Marx looked at the alienation and straight-up suffering endured by factory workers of his day—they were crammed into unsafe factories, and they made products they themselves couldn't afford to buy—and decided there had to be a better way to organize society.

The vision he came up with in the *Communist Manifesto* predicted a world where instead of a few rich capitalists owning the equipment we rely on to make the products we need, everyone could share that property in common. He was a little vague on the particulars of this future communist world, but he was super specific about the problems of the current capitalist one—and he was so convincing that millions have rejected capitalism and launched communist revolutions.

It might seem farfetched to imagine that the political and economic system we live under could undergo massive upheavals in our own lifetime, but it's happened again and again in history. Today in the United States, the richest 1% control more than 50% of the wealth. Marx says this divide between the rich and the poor will only intensify and make conditions for the poor worse until the workers of the world unite and break off their chains.

Maybe someday people at your workplace will organize a strike, refusing to work until conditions change. Will you join them, or will you go in for yet another day on the job? This book will give you ideas, good or bad, about what you might do when that moment comes.

## English Edition of 1888

With Karl Marx having shuffled off his mortal coil, his collaborator and donor Friedrich Engels reviews some basic info about the Manifesto's publication.

The Communist League in 1847 asked Marx (and, Engels misleadingly adds, Engels himself, too) to write a public declaration and explanation of the secret organization's goals—in other words, a manifesto. Karl wrote it in German; it was published in early 1848. The Manifesto was soon translated into several languages.

But the workers in the June uprising of France's 1848 revolution, on whom Marx had pinned some seriously high hopes, were defeated; several communists of the League were hunted down, arrested, and imprisoned; and the League itself was shut down. It seemed the Manifesto was doomed to be just another forgotten work.

Plot twist! The International Working Men's

Association (sometimes called the First International) arose a decade and a half later in an attempt to organize militant workers with different political views. According to the preface, this organization's struggles were matched by a steady increase in acceptance of the Manifesto.

Basically, it looks like everyone is finally agreeing with Karl.

Well, the Manifesto surely got read and translated a bunch more. The preface lists multiple editions—a Russian translation in 1863, a Spanish version in 1886, and plenty of others—and states that the history of the Manifesto's spread reflects the history of the working class movement itself. That's pretty convenient....

Engels distinguishes between socialism and communism and makes it clear that the Manifesto is about the latter. Socialism is a middle class thing, he explains, and you can debate it in what he sarcastically calls respectable company—in other words, among middle- or upper-class folks who want to keep their positions. But communism scares such people: it's a working-class beast, and it aims to change the entire social system completely by ending all class differences forever.

Engels says the Manifesto was his and Marx's joint production, which is actually true. It's just that the League commissioned Karl only, and now most sources, including us, only give the famous guy's name as the author.

Engels goes on to say that the fundamental idea was Karl's. Then we get a handy paragraph summarizing that basic point.

The basic gist of the Manifesto, Engels says, is that political and intellectual ideas—and therefore all of history—are based on the economic system of the day, and thus on class struggles. Today, he says, the exploited and oppressed proletariat can only free themselves by both overthrowing the rich bourgeoisie and ending economic class altogether.

Engels says he believes the Manifesto's key concept will become as important to the subject of history as Darwin's theory of evolution is to the subject of biology.

The preface states that the Manifesto is still correct in general It says the tract never emphasized the practical steps at the end of Section 2 about how a vanguard state (a temporary form of government) should transition a society to communism, and those steps would have to be different in whatever particular countries become communist in the future.

Also, the critique of socialist literature in Section 3 as well as the comparison of communists (actually the Communist League) to various political parties in Section 4 are out of date, being specific to the time the Manifesto was written.

But since the Manifesto is now a famous document, it should be left unchanged, Engels says. Don't fix it if it ain't broken.

Engels notes this 1888 translation into English was a joint work of himself and Samuel Moore, with a few explanatory footnotes by Engels. That's why it's considered the authorized translation.

Note: Other prefaces later written by Engels tend to follow the same lines as this preface, but they talk about the further spread of Manifesto translations as well as the growing working class movement.

Here it is folks, the famous first line: "A spectre is haunting Europe—the spectre of Communism".

Karl says that everyone from the Pope to German policemen (he had some trouble with those coming after him) is fighting this spectre or ghost that is menacing the continent.

Furthermore, politicians are trying to make each other look bad by calling each other communists.

This means that all European political powers agree that communism is a great power, too, Karl says. Yeah, he's exaggerating here, but what's the point of writing a manifesto if you're not going to use some rhetorical devices? Plus, who wants to get in a political movement that isn't fabulous?

Karl thinks it's totally time for communists to openly publish their ideas and aims in order to oppose these false conceptions of communism by bringing out the real story, which is to be translated into many languages. (And indeed, it eventually was.)

Another famous line: "The history of all hitherto existing society is the history of class struggles" (Section1.1). In other words, rich people, poor or enslaved people, and those in the middle have been duking it out ever since society began.

These fights between oppressor and oppressed—whether during the Roman Empire, feudal Europe, or other times—result in either a revolutionary rebuilding of all society or ruin for everyone. Sounds fun.

So, about the bourgeoisie—wait, who are they? They're an economic class that developed, toward the end of feudalism, from the citizens of towns who were neither aristocrats (lords, knights, etc.) nor serfs (peasants who were basically enslaved). These people successfully built up businesses, becoming upper class—a.k.a. rich people—who controlled capital. That makes them capitalists who control the means of production and exchange (more on that soon). See our "Characters" section for a fuller explanation of these peeps.

The rise of the bourgeoisie hasn't changed anything about class struggle, Marx says. It has only established new forms of it and made it a lot more obvious.

On the opposite side of the bourgeoisie is the proletariat. Who are these folks? They're workers who are paid wages. See our "Characters" section for a fuller explanation.

Back to the bourgeoisie. As feudalism—the system of aristocracy versus serfs—was collapsing, the discovery of the Americas by Europeans and the colonial trade increased the bourgeoisie's power rapidly. Basically, colonialism gave the bourgeoisie new markets and resources for their businesses.

Marx is going into full history-teacher mode here. The way industry was organized in the medieval period, with closed guilds, could not keep up with the growing wants of the new marketplaces. So the manufacturing industry arose to supply the wants. Even that wasn't enough, so steam and machinery came along to further revolutionize industrial production.

The Industrial Revolution made new millionaires (the leaders of giant industrial workforces) out of much of the bourgeoisie.

Thus, Marx concludes, the bourgeoisie results from a long course of revolutions in the modes of production and exchange.

What the heck are modes of production and exchange? Well, comrade, production is building products like iPhones, and circulation is sort of managing their distribution—and we're not talking about the way truck drivers haul loads, but instead about the way banks manage this stuff by investing. (Marx thinks of investing as something like gambling or manipulation.)

As the bourgeoisie developed, it won various political gains, often helping the absolute monarchs (kings and queens) by serving as a balancing factor against the aristocratic nobility, which the monarchs had to keep in check. However, now (1848 and today) the bourgeoisie is the most powerful force in the world.

Indeed, Marx says, the bourgeoisie has played a revolutionary role in history. This is a startling line, comrade, because usually communists think of the workers as the revolutionaries. But Marx is talking about the past, about the bourgeoisie ending the medieval period's feudalism.

Whenever they gained power, the bourgeoisie was able to replace the feudal connections between people with the connection of self-interest and money.

In other words, instead of the belief that aristocrats were naturally superior to serfs, for example, the profit motive has now become the principle organizing relationship. Everything boils down to money.

The bourgeoisie took away the honor of occupations, such as physician or poet, and made them, again, all about profit—their work is nothing more than wage-labor, an important term you can read more about in the "Symbols, Imagery, Allegory" section.

The bourgeoisie built wonders far surpassing the pyramids and other ancient monuments and did a bunch of other impressive stuff.

That business is competition requires the bourgeoisie to constantly innovate (see the "Competition" theme for more)—indeed, to revolutionize everything about production. These changes sweep away the familiar, including opinions and relationships, as business is conducted. It's all about the moolah.

The need for a constantly expanding market (new customers, for instance) chases the bourgeoisie around the globe and makes them exploit, or take advantage of, everyone. The bourgeoisie removes what's unique about each nation, reshapes faraway countries in its own image, and uses various nations' natural resources (like oil, for example) for their own purpose: profit.

The requirements of business have concentrated populations into the cities and made undeveloped countries dependent on developed ones. Laws and taxes have become more and more unified in organization. What is unique is dying away; everything is becoming capitalist—money is the bottom line everywhere.

So, Marx sums up, the means of production (factories, for example), which are the foundation of the bourgeoisie, began their development under feudalism and eventually grew so much that feudalism had to collapse and give way to capitalism's rule.

There is a similar change going on before our eyes, Karl continues. The history of industry has been about the bourgeoisie's massive forces of production breaking apart old property relations and establishing new ones. Increasingly severe economic recessions and depressions are the absurd consequence of too much production taking place. But there is another consequence of this growth of capital, or the extra wealth that allows for the creation of more wealth rather than just paying bills (see "Symbols, Imagery, Allegory" for more): the growth of the proletariat, which will overthrow the bourgeoisie, just as the bourgeoisie overthrew feudalism.

The proletariat is a class of laborers who must find work to live but who can only find work when it financially benefits the bourgeoisie. These workers have to sell themselves to the bourgeoisie and are treated like just another commodity, or just another thing for sale. Example: getting fired simply because a company is cutting expenses. Sad face.

Due to the division of labor and the increased use of machinery, workers have become mere cogs in the machine. Their jobs are not personal any longer; they don't have the opportunity to personalize their work. They're stuck in factories and ordered around like soldiers.

As soon as the worker is finished at the factory and paid, more members of the bourgeoisie, such as the landlord and shopkeeper, demand his or her money.

The members of the lower middle class, such as tradespeople, fall into the proletariat (the lower class) because their small amount of capital isn't enough to compete against the large capitalists.

The proletariat goes through stages of development, comrade. First individual workers, then the workpeople at an individual factory, and eventually more and more workers elsewhere retaliate against those who directly exploit them—they smash machinery, they set factories on fire.

But at this stage, the proletariat is still made up of various groups competing against one another. The bourgeoisie finds ways to profit from the proletariat's competition against itself.

But over time, the proletariat, increasing in number, grows stronger from its repeated conflicts with the bourgeoisie and from shared frustrations over fluctuations in their pay. They create labor unions to try to increase their bargaining power.

Sometimes the contest between proletariat and the bourgeoisie breaks out into riots. The real victory of these various battles is that the workers, despite their differences, join together more and more as a force standing against the bourgeoisie.

That capitalism causes competition between workers for jobs, however, is a fact that continues to divide them. Still, the proletariat keeps rising up and joining together, even to the point of creating political parties, aided by new technology improving communication and travel.

Competition makes the bourgeoisie struggle, too. They have to compete against the aristocracy, against each other, and against the bourgeoisie in foreign countries. They ask the proletariat— the bulk of the population—for help, but in doing so, they have to educate them... which is something that will help the proletariat overthrow the bourgeoisie down the road.

Some of the bourgeoisie can't successfully maintain their class status, due to competition, and they become proletarians. Other bourgeoisie (such as Marx and Engels themselves) who understand the historical movement of politics, join the proletariat intentionally to further the revolution.

It's the proletariat who are the revolutionary class, according to Marx. Those in the middle class either try to maintain their position, thus contributing to the capitalist system, or fall into the proletariat by the pressures of competition. The lumpenproletariat, such as beggars, criminals, and drifters, aren't particularly relevant in the class struggle, Marx says.

The proletariat cannot win power without eliminating exploitation altogether. They cannot raise themselves up without changing the structures that allow for exploitation. The struggles of the proletariat will thus lead to the final revolution: the violent overthrow of the bourgeoisie.

To rule, the bourgeoisie has to keep profiting, which requires wage-labor (working for wages, which is what the proletariat does). But wage-labor can only continue as long as the workers fight one another in competition. Instead, Marx says, they're joining together to resist their dangerous workplace conditions. The very foundation of the bourgeoisie is being cut out under its feet.

With a famous image, Marx writes that the bourgeoisie produces its own gravediggers.

Okay here we go. Now Marx talks about the relationship between proletarians and communists, meaning the Communist League who commissioned him to write the Manifesto.

The communists have no interests apart from the proletariat, he says. They point out the common interests of the entire proletariat regardless of country, and they support the whole working class movement's interests. They understand the historical picture and push it forward.

The immediate aim of the communists is to form the proletariat into a massive group, to overthrow the bourgeoisie's supremacy, and to conquer political power.

Now we get into the specifics of communism.

The bourgeoisie objects that communists want to abolish property. But property has always been abolished, Marx says; that the communists want to abolish it is nothing new. The French Revolution abolished feudal property in favor of bourgeoisie property, for example.

The distinguishing feature of the communists is that they want to abolish the private nature of bourgeois property (think of capital and the means of production, like factories and machinery—that's what the communists want to get rid of), which would leave workers the personal product of their labor but not capital with which to exploit others.

In other words, under communism, you're supposed to get to keep your own toothbrush and other personal belongings. But you won't be exploiting a bunch of laborers, forcing them to create toothbrushes for you to sell.

Property under the bourgeois system means exploitation and antagonism between capital and wage-labor. Capital, remember, is the profit of the rich. Wage-labor—that is, the proletariat's work for wages—doesn't create property for laborers; it creates capital for the bourgeoisie.

Here's an example. You might be paid to bake bread at a grocery store for the bourgeoisie to sell. You haven't created bread for yourself to eat; you've created profit for your employer. Now you have to buy food to eat from other members of the bourgeoisie rather than freely eat the bread you just made.

Capital is all that labor added up and taken by the bourgeoisie, rather than the labor serving as means to enrich the lives of the laborers. Abolition of this property system means abolition of bourgeois freedom, of free trade: selling and buying. By free trade, the bourgeoisie meant freedom from feudalism, not freedom for everyone.

Marx says people are horrified by the communists' proposals to abolish private property, but he says it's already been abolished for ninety percent of the population, since the proletariat has been left with the bare minimum of property, just enough to allow them to survive. Communists want to do away with the class character of property and the misery with which the fruits of labor are acquired.

Karl emphasizes again that communism doesn't take away the power of people to acquire and make use of society's products; It only deprives people of the power to turn these products into capital and enslave others with that capital.

The bourgeoisie argues that people will become lazy once bourgeois property is abolished, but Marx says the bourgeoisie is already lazy. It's wage-labor and capital that are to be done away with, not human productivity, comrade.

The bourgeoisie thinks that the disappearance of bourgeois culture means the disappearance of all culture. But for the proletariat, it means ending the culture of having to be a cog in the machine. Bourgeois notions of culture, law, and stuff like that are reflections of the bourgeois mode of production: capitalism. Ruling classes have always been unable to see that their eternal truths are merely reflections of their own class.

Now we get even more extreme. Marx says that people get angry with the communist proposal to abolish the family. Once again, though, communists are referring to the bourgeois family, which is founded on capital and self-interest. The proletariat practically has no family (there's no time for it, and no money), and one result is prostitution. Once capital vanishes, proper relations between people will exist.

Similarly, communists aim to do away with bourgeois education by rescuing education from the ruling class. The bourgeoisie has turned family and education into commerce.

The bourgeoisie protest that communists would introduce a community of women. Basically, that means they think communists want women to be sexually available to the entire community rather than married or otherwise unavailable. But the bourgeoisie, Marx says, see their wives as mere means of production and imagine that because communists want to share the means of production, they must want to make women common to all. But the communist idea, Marx says, is to end the status of women being little production factories in the first place.

Whereas the bourgeoisie is used to seducing each other's wives—and to going to prostitutes—the communists would end the need for prostitution. And besides, he adds, a community of women has nearly always existed to some extent. See the "Women and Femininity" theme for more.

The communists are accused of wanting to abolish countries and nationalities. But, Marx says, the proletariat has no country. National differences and antagonisms are disappearing due to business and the world market, and the coming supremacy of the proletariat will cause nationalities to disappear even faster, since the revolution requires unity from the proletariat to succeed. Hostilities between nations will end, comrade.

Accusations against communism coming from religious, philosophical, or ideological standpoints are not worth consideration, Marx says. Well, that's one way to deal with your opponents.

Anyway, Marx says people's ideas change due to system-wide changes in production, not the other way around. When production changes, ideas change. But all past ideas have developed in the context of class exploitation, so communism is the most radical idea, as the proletarian revolution will end exploitation and thus exploitation-based ideas altogether.

Marx announces that he's sick of talking about the bourgeois objections to communism. So now he's going to get into what his guys, the proletariat, should do once they're in charge.

The proletariat should use its political power to take capital from the bourgeoisie, centralize the means of production into the hands of the State (the proletarians organized as a temporary ruling government, a.k.a. a vanguard state), and increase total production as quickly as possible.

The measures a proletarian State will take will differ from country to country, but Marx outlines ten general steps that there might be. They involve putting credit, communication, transport, the means of production (factories, for example), and more into the hands of the State as inheritance and ownership of land are abolished, taxes are increased, and free education is provided to all.

Once this program ends class distinctions, the power of the proletariat will cease to be political power, because political power is nothing more than the organized power to oppress. And all oppression is class oppression, according to Marx.

In place of the bourgeois society, with all its class antagonisms, people will associate under the principle that freedom for any particular person to develop is the same as the freedom for all to develop.

In this section, Marx clarifies how his and the Communist League's communism differs from the socialism or communism of others.

First, he takes on the aristocrats who advocated for feudal socialism. Basically, as feudalism was coming to an end, the aristocrats were threatened by the rise of the bourgeoisie. So the aristocrats wrote attacks against them and made offerings to the proletariat, hoping for the support of the masses.

But the feudal aristocrats, according to Marx, didn't realize that their rule happened under different forms of production that were now gone.

The aristocrats accused the bourgeoisie of creating a revolutionary proletariat and working against their interests.

Clerical Socialism and Christian asceticism were nothing more than religious ways of approving of the aristocracy.

Next up on Marx's hit list is petty-bourgeois socialism. The petty bourgeoisie is sort of like the middle class today. They were threatened with losing their position and being turned into proletarians. So they advocated for reforms to the system that might help them improve their lives for the time being, but they didn't advocate for revolution—not for anything that would fundamentally alter the system and cause them to lose their status.

The petty-bourgeois writers were sometimes great at criticizing the economic theories of the upper class, but in the final analysis, they didn't want any fundamental changes. The economic views of liberals and the Democratic Party would generally be the example of the petty bourgeoisie outlook in the United States today.

Now Marx gets to German Socialism, also known as True Socialism. These guys, according to him, were philosophers or book-smart people who took on French communist ideas but didn't pay attention to the context of the French Revolution. Instead of understanding the specifics of France, these Germans made the French writings conform to the ideas of their German philosophers. Marx criticizes specific works of the German Socialists and basically says that the authors sucked the revolutionary life out of the French writings and talked about grand philosophical fantasies instead of the actual revolution.

As the German bourgeoisie arose against the aristocrats, German Socialism had a chance to attack, but instead it wound up misunderstanding everything and promoting grand-sounding notions about the ideal German man, who was more of a middle-class person than a proletarian. So much for German Socialism.

Okay, we're moving right along to Conservative or Bourgeois Socialism. Those promoting this view were members of the bourgeoisie who were just offering reforms in order to keep the proletarians' pitchforks away. It's similar to the petty-bourgeois socialism described above. Marx sums these views up as saying that the bourgeoisie is to stay bourgeois, and that's somehow supposed to benefit the proletariat.

Finally, Marx asks us to look at Critical-Utopian socialism or communism, and we say, "Okay." This school of thought basically consisted of writers who understood the problems with capitalism quite well but believed the solution was to form ideal little communities where people could live as communists. They effectively supported the bourgeoisie by rejecting revolution in favor of peaceful, experimental societies that were doomed to failure.

At least, Marx says, the Critical-Utopians offered good criticisms of capitalism. But they didn't understand that the entire working class had to be supported to create real change.

Final section!

Marx starts by listing the parties the Communist League supports in various countries as a matter of tactics, but he emphasizes that they always reserve the right to criticize any party and will always bring the question of abolishing (bourgeois) property to the forefront.

The communists even support the bourgeoisie in some cases, such as when the bourgeoisie opposes the aristocracy, since it's the aristocracy that has to be taken down first.

Marx says Germany deserves particular focus because the bourgeois revolution against the aristocracy about to happen there will soon lead to proletarian revolution.

The Manifesto concludes by saying that the communists do not wish to hide their views and goals. They openly state that their goals can only be accomplished by the forcible overthrow of all existing social conditions.

The ruling class should tremble at the coming communist revolution.

The proletarians have nothing to lose but their chains, and they have a world to win.

And here's the famous last line, which is entirely capitalized (pun totally intended): WORKING MEN OF ALL COUNTRIES, UNITE!

[i] A reference to the movement for a reform of the electoral law which, under the pressure of the working class, was passed by the British House of Commons in 1831 and finally endorsed by the House of Lords in June, 1832. The reform was directed against monopoly rule of the landed and finance aristocracy and opened the way to Parliament for the representatives of the industrial bourgeoisie. Neither workers nor the petty-bourgeois were allowed electoral rights, despite assurances they would.

[ii] The famous final phrase of the Manifesto, "Working Men of All Countries, Unite!", in the original German is: "Proletarier aller Länder, vereinigt euch!" Thus, a more correct translation would be "Proletarians of all countries, Unite!"

"Workers of the World, Unite. You have nothing to lose but your chains!" is a popularisation of the last three sentences, and is not found in any official translation. Since this English translation was approved by Engels, we have kept the original intact.